HORRiD HENRY'S HAUNTED HOUSE

Francesca Simon spent her childhood on the beach in California, and then went to Yale and Oxford Universities to study medieval history and literature. She now lives in London with her family. She has written over 45 books and won the Children's Book of the Year in 2008 at the Galaxy British Book Awards for *Horrid Henry and the Abominable Snowman*.

Also by Francesca Simon

Don't Cook Cinderella
Helping Hercules

Spider School
Illustrated by Tony Ross

The Topsy-Turvies
Illustrated by Emily Bolam

There is a complete list of **Horrid Henry** titles
at the end of the book.
Horrid Henry is also available on audio CD and
digital download, all read by Miranda Richardson.

Visit Horrid Henry's website at
www.horridhenry.co.uk for competitions,
games, gownloads and a monthly newsletter

HORRID HENRY'S HAUNTED HOUSE

Francesca Simon

Illustrated by Tony Ross

Orion
Children's Books

For Mary Gibson,
Head teacher, Yerbury School.
And for Joshua,
who always has such brilliant ideas,
with love and thanks

CONTENTS

1

HORRID HENRY

AND THE
COMFY BLACK CHAIR

Ah, Saturday! Best day of the week, thought Horrid Henry, flinging off the covers and leaping out of bed. No school! No homework! A day of TV heaven! Mum and Dad liked sleeping in on a Saturday. So long as Henry and Peter were quiet they could watch TV until Mum and Dad woke up.

Horrid Henry could picture it now. He would stretch out in the comfy black chair, grab the remote control, and switch on the TV. All his favourite shows were on today: *Rapper Zapper, Mutant*

Max, and *Gross-Out*. If he hurried he would be just in time for *Rapper Zapper*.

He thudded down the stairs and flung open the sitting room door. A horrible sight met his eyes.

There, stretched out on the comfy black chair and clutching the remote control, was his younger brother, Perfect Peter.

Henry gasped. How could this be? Henry always got downstairs first. The TV was already on. But it was not switched to *Rapper Zapper*. A terrible

tinkly tune trickled out of the TV.
Oh no! It was the world's most boring
show, *Daffy and her Dancing Daisies*.

"Switch the channel!" ordered Henry.
"*Rapper Zapper*'s on."

"That's a horrid, nasty programme,"
said Perfect Peter, shuddering. He held
tight to the remote.

"I said switch the channel!" hissed
Henry.

"I won't!" said Peter. "You know the
rules. The first one downstairs gets to sit
in the comfy black chair and decides
what to watch. And I want to watch
Daffy."

Henry could hardly believe his ears.
Perfect Peter was . . . refusing to obey an
order?

"NO!" screamed Henry. "I hate that
show. I want to watch *Rapper Zapper*!"

"Well, I want to watch *Daffy*," said
Perfect Peter.

"But that's a baby show," said Henry.

"Dance, my daisies, dance!" squealed the revolting Daffy.

"La, la la la la!" trilled the daisies.

"La, la la la la!" sang Peter.

"Baby, baby!" taunted Henry. If only he could get Peter to run upstairs crying then *he* could get the chair.

"Peter is a baby, Peter is a baby!" jeered Henry.

Peter kept his eyes glued to the screen.

Horrid Henry could stand it no longer. He pounced on Peter, snatched the remote, and pushed Peter onto the floor. He was Rapper Zapper liquidating a pesky android.

"AAAAAH!" screamed Perfect Peter. "MUUUMMM!"

Horrid Henry leaped into the comfy black chair and switched channels.

"Grrrrrrr!" growled Rapper Zapper, blasting a baddie.

"DON'T BE HORRID, HENRY!" shouted Mum, storming through the door. "GO TO YOUR ROOM!"

"NOOOO!" wailed Henry. "Peter started it!"

"NOW!" screamed Mum.

"La, la la la la!" trilled the Daisies.

★

BUZZZZZZZZZ.

Horrid Henry switched off the alarm. It was six a.m. the following Saturday. Henry was taking no chances. Even if he had to grit his teeth and watch *Rise and Shine* before *Gross-Out* started it was worth it. And he'd seen the coming attractions for today's *Gross-Out*: who could eat the most cherry pie in five minutes while blasting the other contestants with a goo-shooter. Henry couldn't wait.

There was no sound from Peter's room. Ha, ha, thought Henry. He'll have to sit on the lumpy sofa and watch what *I* want to watch.

Horrid Henry skipped into the sitting room. And stopped.

"Remember, children, always eat with a knife and fork!" beamed a cheerful presenter. It was *Manners with Maggie*. There was Perfect Peter in his slippers

and dressing gown, stretched out on
the comfy black chair. Horrid Henry
felt sick. Another Saturday ruined!
He had to watch *Gross-Out*! He just
had to.

Horrid Henry was just about to push
Peter off the chair when he stopped.
Suddenly he had a brilliant idea.

"Peter! Mum and Dad want to see
you. They said it's urgent!"

Perfect Peter leaped off the comfy
black chair and dashed upstairs.

Tee hee, thought Horrid Henry.
ZAP!

"Welcome to *GROSS-OUT!*" shrieked the presenter, Marvin the Maniac. "Boy, will you all be feeling sick today! It's GROSS! GROSS! GROSS!"

"Yeah!" said Horrid Henry. This was great!

Perfect Peter reappeared.

"They didn't want me," said Peter. "And they're cross because I woke them up."

"They told me they did," said Henry, eyes glued to the screen.

Peter stood still.

"Please give me the chair back, Henry."

Henry didn't answer.

"I had it first," said Peter.

"Shut up, I'm trying to watch," said Henry.

"Ewwwwww, gross!" screamed the TV audience.

"I was watching *Manners with Maggie*,"

said Peter. "She's showing how to eat soup without slurping."

"Tough," said Henry. "Oh, gross!" he chortled, pointing at the screen.

Peter hid his eyes.

"Muuuuummmmmmmmm!" shouted Peter. "Henry's being mean to me!"

Mum appeared in the doorway.

She looked furious.

"Henry, go to your room!" shouted Mum. "We were trying to sleep. Is it too much to ask to be left in peace one morning a week?"

"But Peter —"

Mum pointed to the door.

"Out!" said Mum.

"It's not fair!" howled Henry, stomping off.

ZAP!

"And now Kate, our guest manners expert, will demonstrate the proper way to butter toast."

Henry slammed the door behind him as hard as he could. Peter had got the comfy black chair for the very last time.

BUZZZZZZ.

Horrid Henry switched off the alarm. It was two a.m. the *following* Saturday.

The *Gross-Out* Championships were on in the morning. He grabbed his pillow and duvet and sneaked out of the room. He was taking no chances. Tonight he would *sleep* in the comfy black chair. After all, Mum and Dad had never said how *early* he could get up.

Henry tiptoed out of his room into the hall.

All quiet in Peter's room.

All quiet in Mum and Dad's.

Henry crept down the stairs and carefully opened the sitting room door. The room was pitch black. Better not turn on the light, thought Henry. He felt his way along the wall until his fingers touched the back of the comfy black chair. He felt around the top. Ah, there was the remote. He'd sleep with that under his pillow, just to be safe.

Henry flung himself onto the chair and landed on something lumpy.

"AHHHHHHHHH!" screamed
Henry.

"AHHHHHHHHH!" screamed the
Lump.

"HELP!" screamed Henry and the
Lump.

Feet pounded down the stairs.

"What's going on down there?"
shouted Dad, switching on the light.

Henry blinked.

"Henry jumped on my head!" snivelled a familiar voice beneath him.

"Henry, what are you doing?" said Dad. "It's two o'clock in the morning!"

Henry's brain whirled. "I thought I heard a burglar so I crept down to keep watch."

"Henry's lying!" said Peter, sitting up. "He came down because he wanted the comfy black chair."

"Liar!" said Henry. "And what were *you* doing down here?"

"I couldn't sleep and I didn't want to wake you, Dad," said Peter. "So I came down as quietly as I could to get a drink of water. Then I felt sleepy and lay down for a moment. I'm very sorry, Dad, it will never happen again."

"All right," said Dad, stifling a yawn. "From now on, you are not to come down here before seven a.m. or there will be no TV for a week! Is that clear?"

"Yes, Dad," said Peter.

"Yeah," muttered Henry.

He glared at Perfect Peter.

Perfect Peter glared at Horrid Henry. Then they both went upstairs to their bedrooms and closed the doors.

"Goodnight!" called Henry cheerfully. "My, I'm sleepy."

But Henry did not go to bed. He needed to think.

He *could* wait until everyone was asleep and sneak back down. But what if he got caught? No TV for a week would be unbearable.

But what if he missed the *Gross-Out* Championships? And never found out if Tank Thomas or Tapioca Tina won the day? Henry shuddered. There had to be a better way.

Ahh! He had it! He would set his clock ahead and make sure he was first down. Brilliant! *Gross-Out* here I come, he thought.

But wait. What if Peter had the *same* brilliant idea? That would spoil everything. Henry had to double-check.

Henry opened his bedroom door. The coast was clear. He tiptoed out and sneaked into Peter's room.

There was Peter, sound asleep. And there was his clock. Peter hadn't changed the time. Phew.

And then Henry had a truly wicked idea. It was so evil, and so horrid, that for a moment even he hesitated. But hadn't Peter been horrible and selfish, stopping Henry watching his favourite shows? He certainly had. And wouldn't it be great if Peter got into trouble, just for once?

Perfect Peter rolled over. "La, la la la la," he warbled in his sleep.

That did it. Horrid Henry moved Peter's clock an hour ahead. Then Henry sneaked downstairs and turned up the TV's volume as loud as it would go. Finally, he opened Mum and Dad's door, and crept back to bed.

"IT'S GROW AND SHOW! THE VEGETABLE SHOW FOR TINIES! JUST LOOK AT ALL THESE LOVELY VEGETABLES!"

The terrible noise boomed through the house, blasting Henry out of bed.

"HENRY!" bellowed Dad. "Come here this instant!"

Henry sauntered into his parents' bedroom.

"What is it?" he asked, yawning loudly.

Mum and Dad looked confused.

"Wasn't that you watching TV downstairs?"

"No," said Henry, stretching. "I was asleep."

Mum looked at Dad.

Dad looked at Mum.

"You mean *Peter* is downstairs watching TV at six a.m.?"

Henry shrugged.

"Send Peter up here this minute!" said Dad.

For once Henry did not need to be asked twice. He ran downstairs and burst into the sitting room.

"I grew carrots!"

"I grew string beans!"

"Peter! Mum and Dad want to see you right away!" said Henry.

Peter didn't look away from *Grow and Show.*

"PETER! Dad asked me to send you up!"

"You're just trying to trick me," said Peter.

"You'd better go or you'll be in big trouble," said Henry.

"Fool me once, shame on you. Fool me twice, shame on me," said Peter. "I'm not moving."

"Now, just look at all these beautiful tomatoes Timmy's grown," squealed the TV.

"Wow," said Peter.

"Don't say I didn't warn you," said Henry.

"PETER!" bellowed Dad. "NO TV FOR A MONTH! COME HERE THIS MINUTE!"

Perfect Peter burst into tears. He jumped from the chair and crept out of the room.

Horrid Henry sauntered over to the comfy black chair and stretched out. He picked up the remote and switched channels.

ZAP!

Rapper Zapper stormed into the spaceship and pulverized some alien slime.

"Way to go, Rapper Zapper!" shrieked Horrid Henry. Soon *Gross-Out* would be on. Wasn't life sweet?

2

HORRiD HENR
HAUNTED HOUSE

"No way!" shrieked Horrid Henry.
He was not staying the weekend with
his slimy cousin Stuck-up Steve, and that
was that. He sat in the back seat
of the car with his arms folded.

"Yes you are," said Mum.

"Steve can't wait to see you,' said Dad.

This was not exactly true. After Henry
had sprayed Steve with green goo last
Christmas, *and* helped himself to a few of
Steve's presents, Steve had sworn revenge.
Under the circumstances, Henry thought
it would be a good idea to keep out of
Steve's way.

And now Mum had arranged for him to spend the weekend while she and Dad went off on their own! Perfect Peter was staying with Tidy Ted, and he was stuck with Steve.

"It's a great chance for you boys to become good friends," she said. "Steve is a very nice boy."

"I feel sick," said Henry, coughing.

"Stop faking," said Mum. "You were well enough to play football all morning."

"I'm too tired," said Henry, yawning.

"I'm sure you'll get plenty of rest at Aunt Ruby's," said Dad firmly.

"I'M NOT GOING!" howled Henry.

Mum and Dad took Henry by the arms, dragged him to Rich Aunt Ruby's door, and rang the bell.

The massive door opened immediately.

"Welcome, Henry," said Rich Aunt

Ruby, giving him a great smacking kiss.

"Henry, how lovely to see you," said Stuck-up Steve sweetly. "That's a very nice second-hand jumper you're wearing."

"Hush, Steve," said Rich Aunt Ruby. "I think Henry looks very smart."

Henry glared at Steve. Thank goodness he'd remembered his Goo-Shooter. He had a feeling he might need it.

"Goodbye, Henry," said Mum. "Be good. Ruby, thank you so much for having him."

"Our pleasure," lied Aunt Ruby.

The great door closed.

Henry was alone in the house with his arch-enemy.

Henry looked grimly at Steve. What a horrible boy, he thought.

Steve looked grimly at Henry. What a horrible boy, he thought.

"Why don't you both go upstairs and play in Steve's room till supper's ready?" said Aunt Ruby.

"I'll show Henry where he's sleeping first," said Steve.

"Good idea," said Aunt Ruby.

Reluctantly, Henry followed his cousin up the wide staircase.

"I bet you're scared of the dark," said Steve.

"'Course I'm not," said Henry.

"That's good," said Steve. "This is my room," he added, opening the door to an enormous bedroom. Horrid Henry stared longingly at the shelves filled to bursting with zillions of toys and games.

"Of course all *my* toys are brand new. Don't you dare touch anything," hissed Steve. "They're all mine and only *I* can play with them."

Henry scowled. When he was king he'd use Steve's head for target practice.

They continued all the way to the top. Goodness, this old house was big, thought Henry.

Steve opened the door to a large attic bedroom, with brand new pink and blue flowered wallpaper, a four-poster bed, an enormous polished wood wardrobe, and two large windows.

"You're in the haunted room," said Steve casually.

"Great!" said Henry. "I love ghosts." It would take more than a silly ghost to frighten *him*.

"Don't believe me if you don't want to," said Steve. "Just don't blame me when the ghost starts wailing."

"You're nothing but a big fat liar," said Henry. He was sure Steve was lying. He was absolutely sure Steve was lying.

He was one million percent sure that Steve was lying.

He's just trying to pay me back for Christmas, thought Henry.

Steve shrugged. "Suit yourself. See that stain on the carpet?"

Henry looked down at something brownish.

"That's where the ghost vaporized," whispered Steve. "Of course if you're too scared to sleep here ..."

Henry would rather have walked on hot coals than admit being scared to Steve.

He yawned, as if he'd never heard anything so boring.

"I'm looking forward to meeting the ghost," said Henry.

"Good," said Steve.

"Supper, boys!" called Aunt Ruby.

Henry lay in bed. Somehow he'd survived the dreadful meal and Stuck-up Steve's bragging about his expensive clothes, toys and trainers. Now here he was, alone in the attic at the top of the house. He'd jumped into bed, carefully avoiding the faded brown patch on the floor. He was sure it was just spilled cola or something, but just in case . . .

Henry looked around him. The only thing he didn't like was the huge wardrobe opposite the bed. It loomed up in the darkness at him. You could hide a body in that wardrobe, thought Henry, then rather wished he hadn't.

"Oooooooooh."

Henry stiffened.

Had he just imagined the sound of someone moaning?

Silence.

Nothing, thought Henry, snuggling down under the covers. Just the wind.

"Oooooooooh."

This time the moaning was a fraction louder. The hairs on Henry's neck stood up. He gripped the sheets tightly.

"Haaaaaahhhhhhh."

Henry sat up.

"Haaaaaaaaahhhhhhhhhhh."

The ghostly breathy moaning sound was not coming from outside. It appeared to be coming from inside the giant wardrobe.

Quickly, Henry switched on the bed-side light.

What am I going to do? thought Henry. He wanted to run screaming to his aunt.

But the truth was, Henry was too frightened to move.

Some dreadful moaning thing was inside the wardrobe.

Just waiting to get *him*.

And then Horrid Henry remembered who he was. Leader of a pirate gang. Afraid of nothing (except injections).

I'll just get up and check inside that wardrobe, he thought. Am I a man or a mouse?

Mouse! he thought.

He did not move.

"Oooooooooaaaaahhhhhh," moaned

the THING. The unearthly noises were getting louder.

Shall I wait here for IT to get me, or shall I make a move first? thought Henry. Silently, he reached under the bed for his Goo-Shooter.

Then slowly, he swung his feet over the bed. Tiptoe. Tiptoe. Tiptoe.

Holding his breath, Horrid Henry stood outside the wardrobe.

"HAHAHAHAHAHAHAHHA!"

Henry jumped. Then he flung open the door and fired.

SPLAT!

"HAHAHAHAHAHAHAHAHAH AHAHAughhhhhhh –"

The wardrobe was empty.

Except for something small and greeny-black on the top shelf.

It looked like – it was!

Henry reached up and took it.

It was a cassette player. Covered in green goo.

Inside was a tape. It was called "Dr Jekyll's Spooky Sounds."

Steve, thought Horrid Henry grimly. REVENGE!

"Did you sleep well, dear?" asked Aunt Ruby at breakfast.

"Like a log," said Henry.

"No strange noises?" asked Steve.

"No," smiled Henry sweetly. "Why, did you hear something?"

42

Steve looked disappointed. Horrid Henry kept his face blank. He couldn't wait for the evening.

Horrid Henry spent a busy day.
He went ice-skating.
He went to the cinema.
He played football.

After supper, Henry went straight to bed.

"It's been a lovely day," he said. "But I'm tired. Goodnight, Aunt Ruby. Goodnight, Steve."

"Goodnight, Henry," said Ruby.

Steve ignored him.

But Henry did not go to his bedroom. Instead he sneaked into Steve's.

He wriggled under Steve's bed and lay there, waiting.

Soon Steve came into the room. Henry resisted the urge to reach out and seize Steve's skinny leg. He had something much scarier in mind.

He heard Steve putting on his blue bunny pyjamas and jumping into bed. Henry waited until the room was dark.

Steve lay above him, humming to himself.

"Dooby dooby dooby do," sang Steve.

Slowly, Henry reached up, and ever so slightly, poked the mattress.

Silence.

"Dooby dooby dooby do," sang Steve, a little more quietly.

Henry reached up and poked the mattress again.

Steve sat up.

Then he lay back.

Henry poked the mattress again, ever so slightly.

"Must be my imagination," muttered Steve.

Henry allowed several moments to pass. Then he twitched the duvet.

"Mummy," whimpered Steve.

Jab! Henry gave the mattress a definite poke.

"AHHHHHHHHHHHH!" screamed Steve. He leaped up and ran out of the room. "MUMMY! HELP! MONSTERS!"

Henry scrambled out of the room and ran silently up to his attic. Quick as he could he put on his pyjamas, then clattered noisily back down the stairs to Steve's.

Aunt Ruby was on her hands and knees, peering under the bed. Steve was shivering and quivering in the corner.

"There's nothing here, Steve," she said firmly.

"What's wrong?" asked Henry.

"Nothing," muttered Steve.

"You're not *scared* of the dark, are you?" said Henry.

"Back to bed, boys," said Aunt Ruby. She left the room.

"Ahhhhh, Mummy, help! Monsters!" mimicked Henry, sticking out his tongue.

"MUM!" wailed Steve. "Henry's being horrid!"

47

"GO TO BED, BOTH OF YOU!" shrieked Ruby.

"Watch out for monsters," said Henry.

Steve did not move from his corner.

"Want to swap rooms tonight?" said Henry.

Steve did not wait to be asked twice.

"Oh yes," said Steve.

"Go on up," said Henry. "Sweet dreams."

Steve dashed out of his bedroom as fast as he could.

Tee hee, thought Horrid Henry, pulling Steve's toys down from the shelves. Now, what would he play with first?

Oh, yes. He'd left a few spooky sounds of his own under the attic bed – just in case.

3

HORRiD HENRY'S
SCHOOL FAIR

"Henry! Peter! I need your donations to the school fair NOW!"

Mum was in a bad mood. She was helping Moody Margaret's mum organize the fair and had been nagging Henry for ages to give away some of his old games and toys. Horrid Henry hated giving. He liked getting.

Horrid Henry stood in his bedroom. Everything he owned was on the floor.

"How about giving away those bricks?" said Mum. "You never play with them any more."

"NO!" said Henry. They were bound

to come in useful some day.

"How about some soft toys? When was the last time you played with Spotty Dog?"

"NO!" said Horrid Henry. "He's mine!"

Perfect Peter appeared in the doorway dragging two enormous sacks.

"Here's my contribution to the school fair, Mum," said Perfect Peter.

Mum peeped inside the bags.

"Are you sure you want to give away so many toys?" said Mum.

"Yes," said Peter. "I'd like other children to have fun playing with them."

"What a generous boy you are, Peter," she said, giving him a big hug.

Henry scowled. Peter could give away all his toys, for all Henry cared. Henry wanted to keep everything.

Wait! How could he have forgotten?

Henry reached under his bed and pulled out a large box hidden under a blanket. The box contained all the useless, horrible presents Henry had ever received. Packs of hankies. Vests with ducks on them. A nature guide. Uggh! Henry hated nature. Why would anyone want to waste their time looking at pictures of flowers and trees?

And then, right at the bottom, was the worst present of all. A Walkie-Talkie-

Burpy-Slurpy-Teasy-Weasy Doll. He'd got it for Christmas from a great-aunt he'd never met. The card she'd written was still attached.

Dear Henrietta

I thought this doll would be perfect for a sweet little two-year-old like you! Take good care of your new baby!

Love

Great-Aunt Greta

Even worse, she'd sent Peter something brilliant.

Dear Pete
You must be a teenager by now and too old for toys, so here's £25. Don't spend it all on sweets!
Love
Great-Aunt Greta

Henry had screamed and begged, but Peter got to keep the money, and Henry was stuck with the doll. He was far too embarrassed to try to sell it, so the doll just lived hidden under his bed with all the other rotten gifts.

"Take that," said Henry, giving the doll a kick.

"Mama Mama Mama!" burbled the doll. "Baby burp!"

"Not Great-Aunt Greta's present!" said Mum.

"Take it or leave it," said Henry. "You can have the rest as well."

Mum sighed. "Some lucky children are going to be very happy." She took the hateful presents and put them in the jumble sack.

Phew! He'd got rid of that doll at last! He'd lived in terror of Rude Ralph or Moody Margaret coming over and finding it. Now he'd never have to see that burping slurping long-haired thing again.

Henry crept into the spare room where Mum was keeping all the donated toys and games for the fair. He thought he'd have a quick poke around and see what good stuff would be for sale tomorrow. That way he could make a dash and be first in the queue.

There were rolls of raffle tickets, bottles of wine, the barrel for the lucky dip, and sacks and sacks of toys. Wow, what a hoard! Henry just had to move that rolled up poster out of the way and start rummaging!

Henry pushed aside the poster and then stopped.

I wonder what this is, he thought. I think I'll just unroll it and have a little peek. No harm in that.

Carefully, he untied the ribbon and laid the poster flat on the floor. Then he gasped.

This wasn't jumble. It was the Treasure Map! Whoever guessed where the treasure was hidden always won a fabulous prize. Last year Sour Susan had won a skateboard. The year before Jolly Josh had won a Super Soaker 2000. Boy it sure was worth trying to find that treasure! Horrid Henry usually had at

least five goes. But his luck was so bad
he had never even come close.

Henry looked at the map. There was
the island, with its caves and lagoons, and
the sea surrounding it, filled with whales

and sharks and pirate ships. The map
was divided into a hundred numbered
squares. Somewhere under one of those
squares was an X.

I'll just admire the lovely picture,
thought Henry. He stared and stared.
No X. He ran his hands over the map.
No X.

Henry sighed. It was so unfair!
He never won anything. And this year
the prize was sure to be a Super Soaker
5000.

Henry lifted the map to roll it up.
As he raised the thick paper to the light,
a large, unmistakable X was suddenly
visible beneath square 42.

The treasure was just under the whale's eye.

He had discovered the secret.

"YES!" said Horrid Henry, punching the air. "It's my lucky day, at last!"

But wait. Mum was in charge of the Treasure Map stall. If he was first in the queue and instantly bagged square 42 she was sure to be suspicious. So how could he let a few other children go first, but make sure none of them chose the right square? And then suddenly, he had a brilliant, spectacular idea . . .

"Tra la la la la!" trilled Horrid Henry, as he, Peter, Mum and Dad walked to the school fair.

"You're cheerful today, Henry," said Dad.

"I'm feeling lucky," said Horrid Henry.

He burst into the playground and went straight to the Treasure Map stall. A large queue of eager children keen to pay 20p for a chance to guess had already formed. There was the mystery prize, a large, tempting, Super Soaker-sized box. Wheeee!

Rude Ralph was first in line.

"Psst, Ralph," whispered Henry. "I know where X marks the spot. I'll tell you if you give me 50p."

"Deal," said Ralph.

"92," whispered Henry.

"Thanks!" said Ralph. He wrote his name in square 92 and walked off, whistling.

Moody Margaret was next.

"Pssst, Margaret," whispered Henry. "I know where X marks the spot."

"Where?" said Margaret.

"Pay me 50p and I'll tell you," whispered Henry.

"Why should I trust you?" said
Margaret loudly.

Henry shrugged.

"Don't trust me then, and I'll tell
Susan," said Henry.

Margaret gave Henry 50p.

"2," whispered Horrid Henry.

Margaret wrote her name in square 2, and skipped off.

Henry told Lazy Linda the treasure square was 4.

Henry told Dizzy Dave the treasure square was 100.

Weepy William was told 22.

Anxious Andrew was told 14.

Then Henry thought it was time he bagged the winning square. He made sure none of the children he'd tricked were nearby, then pushed into the queue behind Beefy Bert. His pockets bulged with cash.

"What number do you want, Bert?" asked Henry's mum.

"I dunno," said Bert.

"Hi Mum," said Henry. "Here's my 20p. Hmmm, now where could that treasure be?"

Horrid Henry pretended to study the map.

"I think I'll try 37," he said. "No wait, 84. Wait, wait, I'm still deciding . . ."

"Hurry up Henry," said Mum. "Other children want to have a go."

"Okay, 42," said Henry.

Mum looked at him. Henry smiled at her and wrote his name in the square.

Then he sauntered off.

He could feel that Super Soaker in his hands already. Wouldn't it be fun to spray the teachers!

Horrid Henry had a fabulous day. He threw wet sponges at Miss Battle-Axe in the "Biff a Teacher" stall. He joined in his class square dance. He got a marble in the lucky dip. Henry didn't even scream when Perfect Peter won a box of notelets in the raffle and Henry didn't win anything, despite spending £3 on tickets.

"TIME TO FIND THE WINNER OF THE TREASURE MAP COMPETITION," boomed a voice over the playground. Everyone stampeded to the stall.

Suddenly Henry had a terrible thought. What if Mum had switched the X to a different spot at the last minute? He couldn't bear it. He absolutely

couldn't bear it. He had to have that
Super Soaker!

"And the winning number is . . ."
Mum lifted up the Treasure Map . . .
"42! The winner is – Henry."

"Yes!" screamed Henry.

"What?" screamed Rude Ralph,
Moody Margaret, Lazy Linda, Weepy
William, and Anxious Andrew.

"Here's your prize, Henry," said Mum.

She handed Henry the enormous box.

"Congratulations." She did not look very pleased.

Eagerly, Henry tore off the wrapping paper. His prize was a Walkie-Talkie-Burpy-Slurpy-Teasy-Weasy Doll.

"Mama Mama Mama!" burbled the doll. "Baby Slurp!"

"AAARRGGGHHHH!" howled Henry.

4

HORRID HENRY
MINDS HIS MANNERS

"Henry and Peter! You've got mail!" said Mum.

Henry and Peter thundered down the stairs. Horrid Henry snatched his letter and tore open the green envelope. The foul stink of mouldy socks wafted out.

Yo Henry!

Marvin the Maniac here. You sound just like the kind of crazy guy we want on Gross-Out! Be at TV Centre next Saturday at 9.00 a.m. and gross us out! It's a live broadcast, so anything can happen!

Marvin

"I've been invited to be a contestant on *Gross-Out!*" screamed Henry, dancing up and down the stairs. It was a dream come true. "I'll be shooting it out with Tank Thomas and Tapioca Tina while eating as much ice cream as I can!"

"Absolutely not!" said Mum. "You will not go on that disgusting show!"

"Agreed," said Dad. "That show is revolting."

"It's meant to be revolting!" said Horrid Henry. "That's the point."

"N–O spells no," said Mum.

"You're the meanest, most horrible

parents in the whole world," screamed Henry. "I hate you!" He threw himself on the sofa and wailed. "I WANT TO BE ON *GROSS-OUT*! I WANT TO BE ON *GROSS-OUT*!"

Perfect Peter opened his letter. The sweet smell of lavender wafted out.

Dear Peter,
What a wonderful letter you wrote on the importance of perfect manners! As a reward I would like to invite you to be my special guest on the live broadcast of Manners With Maggie

*next Saturday at TV Centre
at 9:00 a.m.*

*You will be showing the girls and boys
at home how to fold a hankie perfectly,
how to hold a knife and fork elegantly,
and how to eat spaghetti beautifully with
a fork and spoon.*

*I am very much looking forward to
meeting you and to enjoying your lovely
manners in person.*

Sincerely,

Maggie.

"I've been invited to appear on *Manners With Maggie!*" said Peter, beaming.

"That's wonderful, Peter!" said Mum. She hugged him.

"I'm so proud of you," said Dad. He hugged him.

Horrid Henry stopped screaming.

"That's not fair!" said Henry. "If Peter

can be on his favourite TV show why can't I be on mine?"

Mum and Dad looked at each other.

"I suppose he does have a point," said Dad. He sighed.

"And we don't have to tell anyone he's on," said Mum. She sighed.

"All right, Henry. You can be a contestant."

"YIPPEE!" squealed Henry, stomping on the sofa and doing his victory jig. "I'm going to be a star! *Gross-Out* here I come!"

The great day arrived at last. Horrid Henry had been practising so hard with his Goo-Shooter he could hit Perfect Peter's nose at thirty paces. He'd also been practising shovelling ice cream into his mouth as fast as he could, until Mum caught him.

Perfect Peter had been practising so hard folding his hankie that he could do it with one hand. And no one could twirl spaghetti with a spoon as beautifully or hold a knife and fork as elegantly as Perfect Peter.

At nine a.m. sharp, Mum, Henry, and Peter walked into TV Centre. Henry was starving. He'd skipped breakfast, to have more room for all the ice cream he'd be gobbling.

Horrid Henry wore old jeans and dirty trainers. Perfect Peter wore a jacket and tie.

A woman with red hair and freckles rushed up to them with a clipboard.

"Hi, I'm Super Sally. Welcome to TV Centre. I'm sorry boys, we'll have to dash, we're running late. Come with me to the guests' waiting room. You're both on in five minutes."

"Can't I stay with them?" said Mum.

"Parents to remain downstairs in the parents' room," said Super Sally sternly. "You can watch on the monitors there."

"Good luck, boys," said Mum, waving.

Sally stared at Peter as they hurried down the hall.

"Aren't you worried about getting those smart clothes dirty?" said Sally.

Peter looked shocked.

"I *never* get my clothes dirty," he said.

"There's always a first time," chortled Sally. "Here's the waiting room. Studios one and two where you'll be filming are through those doors at the end."

In the room was a sofa and two tables. One, marked *Gross-Out*, was groaning with sweets, crisps and fizzy drinks.

The second, labelled *Manners with Maggie*, was laid with a crisp white cloth. A few dainty vegetables were displayed on a china plate.

Horrid Henry suddenly felt nervous. Today was his day to be a TV star! Had he practised enough? And he was so hungry! His stomach tightened.

"I need a wee," said Horrid Henry.

"Toilets next door," said Super Sally. "Be quick. You're on in one minute."

Perfect Peter didn't feel in the least nervous. Practice made perfect, and he knew he was. What disgusting food, he thought, wandering over to the *Gross-Out* table.

A man wearing combat fatigues dashed into the room.

"Ah, there you are!" he boomed. "Come along! It's your big moment!"

"I'm ready," said Peter, waving his handkerchief.

The man pushed him through the door marked Stage 1.

Henry returned.

A lady in high heels and a pearl necklace poked her head round the door.

"You're on, dear!" said the lady. "Goodness, you look a little untidy. Never mind, can't be helped." And she ushered Henry through the door marked Stage 2.

Henry found himself on a brightly lit stage. He blinked in the brilliant lights.

"Let's give a warm welcome to today's guest!" cried a voice. A *female* voice.

The studio audience exploded into applause.

Henry froze. Who was that woman? Where was Marvin the Maniac?

Something's wrong, he thought. This was not the set of *Gross-Out*. It was a pink and yellow kitchen. Yet it looked vaguely familiar . . .

Meanwhile, on Stage 1, Perfect Peter shrank back in horror as two gigantic children carrying Goo-Shooters and massive bowls of ice cream advanced towards him. A presenter, laughing like a hyena, egged them on.

"You're not Maggie!" said Peter. "And I don't know how to use a —"

"Get him guys!" squealed Marvin the Maniac.

"HELLLLP!" shrieked Peter. SPLAT!

Back on Stage 2, Henry suddenly
realized where he was.

"Now don't be shy, darling!" said the
presenter, walking quickly to Henry and
taking him firmly by the hand. "Peter's
here to show us how to fold a hankie
and how to eat beautifully!" It was
Maggie. From *Manners with Maggie*.

What could Henry do? He was
on live TV! There were the cameras

zooming in on him. If he screamed there'd been a terrible mistake that would ruin the show. And hadn't he heard that the show must go on? Even a dreadful show like *Manners with Maggie*?

Henry strolled onto centre stage, smiling and bowing.

"Now Peter will show us the perfect way to fold a hankie."

Horrid Henry felt a sneeze coming.

"AAAACHOOO!" he sneezed. Then he wiped his nose on his sleeve.

The audience giggled. Maggie looked stunned.

"The ... hankie," she prompted.

"Oh yeah," said Henry, feeling in his pockets. He removed a few crumpled wads of ancient tissue.

"Here, use mine," said Maggie smoothly.

Henry took the beautifully embroidered square of silky cloth and scrunched it into a ball. Then he stuffed it into his pocket.

"Nothing to it," said Henry. "Scrunch and stuff. But why bother with a hankie when a sleeve works so much better?"

Maggie gulped. "Very funny, Peter dear! *We* know he's only joking, don't we, children! Now we'll show the girls and boys –"

But Horrid Henry had noticed the table, set with a chocolate cake and a large bowl of spaghetti. Yummy! And Henry hadn't eaten anything for ages.

"Hey, that cake looks great!" interrupted Henry. He dashed to the table, dug out a nice big hunk and shoved it in his mouth.

"Stop eating!" hissed Maggie. "We haven't finished the hankie demonstration yet!"

But Henry didn't stop.

"Yummy," he said, licking his fingers.

Maggie looked like she was going to faint.

"Show the girls and boys how to use a knife and fork elegantly, Peter," she said, with gritted teeth.

"Nah, a knife and fork slows you

down too much. I *always* eat with my fingers. See?"

Horrid Henry waved his chocolate-covered hands.

"I'm sure it was just the excitement of being on TV that made you forget to offer *me* a slice of cake," prompted Maggie. She gazed in horror at the cake, now with a gaping hole on the side.

"But I want to eat it all myself!" said Horrid Henry. "I'm starving! Get your own cake."

"Now I'm going to teach you the proper way to eat spaghetti," said Maggie stiffly, pretending she hadn't heard. "Which we should have done first, of course, as we do not eat dessert before the main course."

"I do!" said Henry.

"Hold your spoon in your left hand, fork in your right, pick up a teensy tiny amount of spaghetti and twirl twirl twirl.

Let's see if my little helper can do it.
I'm sure he's been practising at home."

" 'Course," lied Henry. How hard
could it be to twirl spaghetti? Henry
picked up his spoon, plunged his fork
into an enormous pile of spaghetti and
started to twirl. The spaghetti flew round
the kitchen. A few strands landed on
Maggie's head.

"Whoops," said Henry. "I'll try again." Before Maggie could stop him he'd seized another huge forkful.

"It keeps falling off," said Henry. "Listen, kids, use your fingers – it's faster." Then Henry scooped a handful of spaghetti and crammed it into his mouth.

"It's good," mumbled Henry, chewing loudly with his mouth open.

"Stop! Stop!" said Maggie. Her voice rose to a polite scream.

"What's wrong?" said Henry, trailing great strings of spaghetti out of his mouth.

Suddenly Henry heard a high-pitched howl. Then Perfect Peter burst onto the set, covered in green goo, followed by whooping children waving Goo-Shooters.

"Maggie! Save me!" shrieked Peter, dropping his shooter and hurling himself

into her arms. "They're trying to make me eat between meals!"

"Get away from me, you horrible child!" screamed Maggie.

It was the Goo-Shooter gang at last! Better late than never, thought Henry.

"Yeee haaa!" Henry snatched Peter's Goo-Shooter, jumped onto the table and sprayed Tapioca Tina, Tank Thomas and most of the audience. Gleefully, they returned fire. Henry took a step back, and stepped into the spaghetti.

SPLAT!

"Help!" screamed Maggie, green goo and spaghetti dripping from her face.

"Help!" screamed Peter, green goo and spaghetti dripping from his hair.

"CUT!" shouted the director.

Horrid Henry was lying on the comfy black chair flicking channels. Sadly, *Manners with Maggie* was no longer on TV since Maggie had been dragged screaming off the set. *Mischief with Mildred* would be on soon. Henry thought he'd give it a try.

HORRiD HENRY BOOKS

For Younger Readers

Colour Books

Horrid Henry's Big Bad Book
Horrid Henry's Wicked Ways
Horrid Henry's Evil Enemies
Horrid Henry Rules the World
Horrid Henry's House of Horrors
Horrid Henry's Dreadful Deeds
Horrid Henry Shows Who's Boss

Joke Books

Horrid Henry's Joke Book
Horrid Henry's Jolly Joke Book
Horrid Henry's Mighty Joke Book
Horrid Henry's Hilariously Horrid Joke Book
Horrid Henry's Double Dare
Moody Margaret Strikes Back

Colour Books

Horrid Henry's Brainbusters
Horrid Henry's Headscratchers
Horrid Henry's Mindbenders
Horrid Henry's Colouring Book
Horrid Henry's Puzzle Book
Horrid Henry's Sticker Book
Horrid Henry's Crazy Crosswords
Horrid Henry's Mad Mazes
Horrid Henry's Wicked Wordsearches
Horrid Henry's Classroom Chaos
Horrid Henry's Holiday Havoc
Horrid Henry Runs Riot

HORRID HENRY

Horrid Henry is dragged to a dance
class, makes some disgusting glop
with Moody Margaret from next door,
discovers he doesn't like camping,
and does his best to get even with
his little brother Peter.

HORRID HENRY
AND THE SECRET CLUB

Horrid Henry gets an injection,
torments his little brother Perfect Peter,
creates havoc at his own birthday party,
and plans sweet revenge when
Moody Margaret won't let him
into her Secret Club.

HORRID HENRY
TRICKS THE TOOTH FAIRY

Horrid Henry tries to trick the
Tooth Fairy, has Moody Margaret
to stay and sends her packing, makes
teachers run screaming from school,
and single-handedly wrecks a wedding.

HORRID HENRY'S
NITS

Horrid Henry has nits! And he's on a
mission to give them to everyone else
too. After that, he can turn his attention
to sabotaging his school trip, ruining his
parents' dinner party and terrorizing
Perfect Peter.

HORRID HENRY
GETS RICH QUICK

Horrid Henry makes sure he gets
the presents he wants for Christmas,
sabotages the school sports day, runs away
from home, and thinks of a brilliant
way to get rich quick.